Theo
At the Park

This book belongs to

_____

who has a great sense of smell, unlike little Theo.

Sandy Creek
NEW YORK

Sandy Creek
NEW YORK

An Imprint of Sterling Publishing
387 Park Avenue South
New York, NY 10016

This 2013 edition published by Sandy Creek.

celessence™
Scent technology by Celessence™

Written by Jaclyn Crupi
Illustrations by Aurélia Verdoux

ISBN 978-1-4351-4723-2

Manufactured in Shenzhen, China
Lot #:
2 4 6 8 10 9 7 5 3 1
04/13

To my own little Theodorable—S.G.

This is Theo. He is usually a
happy dog. He can sniff out
adventure a mile away.

He likes to play with his toys.

He likes to chew on his bone.

He likes to snuggle in his bed.

But this morning something is wrong.
Something is different. Something smells fishy...

Actually, that is the problem. Theo cannot smell anything fishy. He cannot smell anything at all.

Theo has lost his sense of smell! But where has he lost it? Where can it be?

Theo decides to retrace his steps from yesterday.

He boldly heads to the park. Maybe he left his sense of smell there.

Theo strides into the park. He immediately sees a beehive.
Theo is sure he will find his sense of smell here.

He leans in, twitches his nose, and wiggles his nostrils.
He breathes in deeply.

Can you smell the sweet honey scent?

Theo sniffs and whiffs the honey. He takes deep breaths. He takes quick breaths.

But he smells nothing. No odor, no scent,
no fragrance; nothing.
"Where is my sense of smell?" Theo wonders.
"Where could it be?"

Theo looks around the park and has an idea.

Theo races over to a rose bush. He is sure he will be able to smell the flowers.

"Roses have a strong perfume," he thinks.
"They will help me find my sense of smell."
Theo breathes in deeply.

Can you smell the roses' perfume?

Theo sniffs and whiffs the roses. He takes short breaths.
He takes long breaths. But he smells nothing.

No perfume, no odor, no fragrance; nothing.

"Where is my sense of smell?" Theo wonders. "Where could it be?"

Theo sniffs the air one more time and has another idea.

Theo bolts for the ice cream stand. He sees they have strawberry ice cream, his favorite.

He is sure strawberry ice cream will help him get his sense of smell back. Theo leans towards the scoops of ice cream. Theo breathes in deeply.

Can you smell the strawberry ice cream aroma?

Theo sniffs and whiffs the strawberry ice cream. He licks
it. He breathes in and holds his breath. But he smells
nothing. No flavor, no smell, no scent; nothing.

All of this sniffing and whiffing has made Theo tired and
he decides to head home.

Maybe his sense of smell is waiting for him there.
He hopes his dinner is!

Theo heads to his dinner bowl. Suddenly his ears prick up.
Theo sniffs and whiffs his dinner.

He breathes deeply.
Wait, what's that?

It's... He sniffs. He sniffs again but can't smell a thing.

After a long day, Theo is worn out and before he can get his sense of smell back, he has fallen into a deep sleep, snuggled in his bed.

Until he follows his nose next time…